For Harlan

A CITY IS

Hicks Street Rules!

POEMS BY **Norman Rosten**

COLLECTED AND EDITED BY **Patricia Rosten Filan**

ILLUSTRATED BY

Melanie Hope Greenberg

Melanie Hope Greenberg

Henry Holt and Company
New York

Henry Holt and Company, LLC
Publishers since 1866
115 West 18th Street
New York, New York 10011
www.henryholt.com

Henry Holt is a registered trademark of Henry Holt and Company, LLC
Text copyright © 2004 by Patricia Rosten Filan
Illustrations copyright © 2004 by Melanie Hope Greenberg
All rights reserved.
Distributed in Canada by H. B. Fenn and Company Ltd.

Library of Congress Cataloging-in-Publication Data
Rosten, Norman, 1914–1995
A city is / by Norman Rosten; collected and edited by Patricia Rosten Filan;
illustrated by Melanie Hope Greenberg.
p.   cm.
Summary: An illustrated collection of poems about New York City.
1. New York (N.Y.)—Juvenile poetry. 2. City and town life—Juvenile poetry. 3. Children's poetry,
American. [1. City and town life—Poetry. 2. American poetry—Collections.] I. Filan, Patricia Rosten.
II. Greenberg, Melanie Hope, ill. III. Title.
PS3535.O758C58 2004   811'.52—dc22   2003012247

ISBN 0-8050-6793-0 / First Edition—2004 / Designed by Amy Manzo Toth
Printed in the United States of America on acid-free paper. ∞

10 9 8 7 6 5 4 3 2 1

The artist used gouache on 140-pound cold-press watercolor paper
to create the illustrations for this book.

Lots of cities
have rivers.

Is it better for a river
to go around a city
or go under it
or through it?

Has anyone ever seen a river
go *over* it?

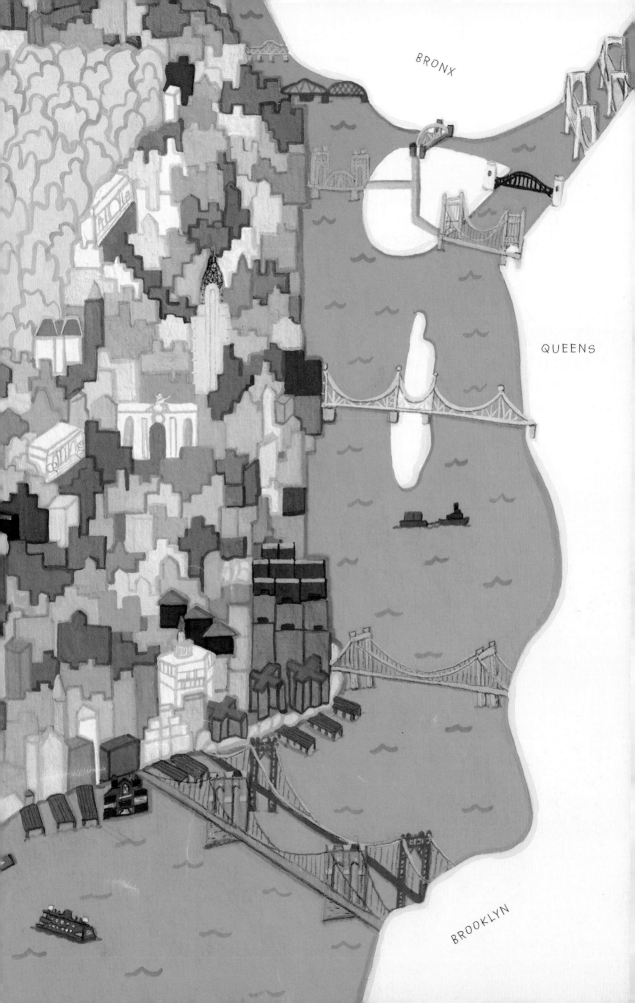

BRONX

QUEENS

BROOKLYN

Ferry to Jersey,
ferry to Staten,
ferry up the river,
or around Manhattan.

Hurry, take the ferry!
By day it's cool,
by night it's starry,
and the whistle's always friendly.

What's a street?
What's an avenue?
Sometimes they cross,
sometimes they never meet
but go on and on
till they come to an end—
to a garden maybe
with a scarecrow waving.

AVENUE D

BARUCH PLACE

COLUMBIA STREET

It's spring!
Kite on a string
sailing in the sky.

People wave their hand,
the kite waves a tail.
It's a happy day
when the kite goes sailing.

Up, up on a skinny string.
Look! It just broke away!
Hope it lands on a soft place
like a pillow, or cloud.

Punch the ball
and run to the base.
Catch the ball
and throw the guy out.

Slide, ya bum!
Honk, honk, outta the way!
C'mon, let's play.
You're out!

In the summer when it rains
the sky gets dark—
we run for cover.

Then the sun comes out.
The birds sing while taking a bath
in puddles and wet grass.
What fun when it rains!

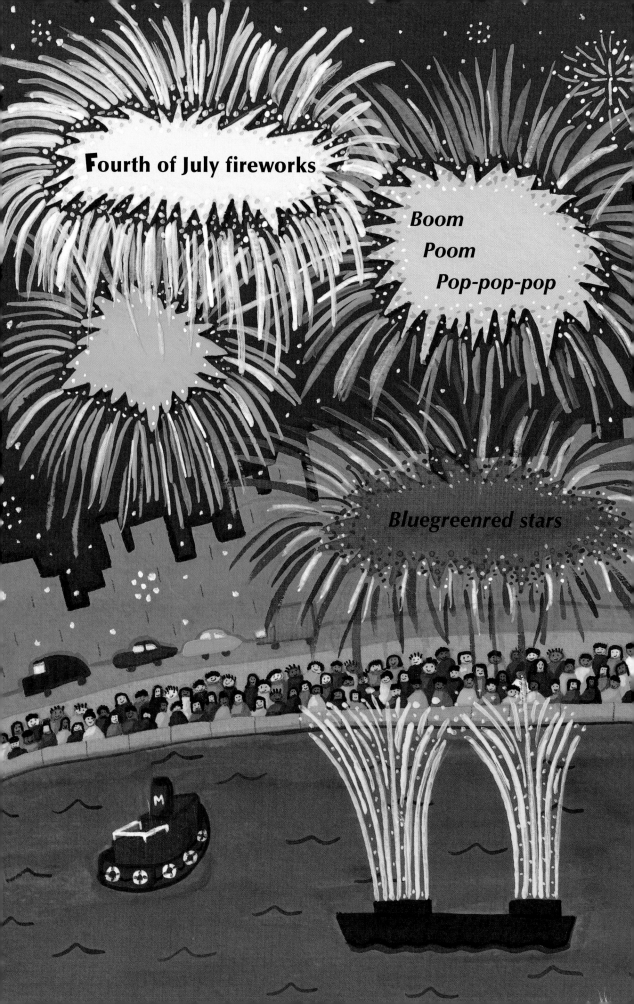

Sometimes I visit the pocket park.

Is that a park you can put in your pocket?

No, no, smarty, it's not *that* small.
   BUT
it can fit (all of it)
between two buildings—
just big enough
for some small shady trees
and a bench to sit and read.

ONE EAST 53RD

TAXI

In the fall
I like the city park most
where the squirrels rush about
burying nuts against the frost,
closing storm windows
wherever their secret houses are. . . .

Snow makes the city
clean and beautiful.

Snow makes the city very quiet—
you can even whisper and be heard.

Plants are covered over
and asleep for the winter.

I feel sorry for the sparrow
shivering on a branch
and a pigeon crossing the street
getting his feet wet.

The winter birds
are huddled together
outside the windows
where snow is falling.

Little cold sparrows
talk to one another:

Will you keep me warm?
You warm me and I'll warm you.
Come close, come closer!

See the clouds
on their way
to New Jersey
or even farther.

They rest for an hour
on a church spire
or a sky-high building
or TV antenna.

A skyscraper
is a place for a star
to rest,
to look its best,
or maybe to take a nap.

While buildings sleep
the moon is drifting
like a toy balloon
over the Brooklyn Bridge.